BECKETT THE BAD BOY

SUITOR'S CROSSING: THE CALDWELLS #4

HALLIE BENNETT

I0619330

Searching for more from Suitor's Crossing?

Check out the Mountain Men of Suitor's Crossing series <u>here</u>[1]!

CHAPTER ONE

BETH DAYTON

An earth-shattering boom shakes City Hall the moment I sit at my desk. The old building is over a hundred years old, and despite undergoing renovations and upgrades over the decades, I pray it's not about to collapse on top of me.

Buried beneath centuries-old rubble is *not* the way I want to go.

Especially when I'm just starting to get my life together.

Moving to Suitor's Crossing to be nearer my friends. Landing a higher-paying job. I've even managed to overcome my cautious nature by hanging out at a motorcycle club's compound on the outskirts of town.

Granted, I'm surrounded by my best friends and their significant others—military veterans, and *not* biker criminals—but it's a step in the right direction.

Death at this point would really suck.

A few of my officemates get up to look out the window, but I remain seated, sharing a look of confusion with Shawna across the room. We're all waiting for an explanation for the sudden noise and subsequent rattling of the building when an insistent hammering echoes through the walls.

"What the—" My question is cut off when the overhead lights blink out, our computers go dark, and alarms start blaring in the hall.

Emergency lights flash.

Sirens whine.

It's like I've been plopped in the middle of an apocalyptic scene of chaos, and I am *not* prepared to survive in a world gone wild, *Mad Max*-style.

Panic sets in as people gather their phones and personal effects from their desks. I should probably get moving, too, but shouldn't we figure out what's going on before running out into god knows what?

"Are you coming?" Shawna has her purse slung over her shoulder and glances toward the hall where groups of City Hall employees are trekking toward the exits—one elevator and a narrow set of stairs.

The elevator was the city's concession to comply with ADA laws since the original layout barred anyone who couldn't climb stairs from accessing the second and third floors, but it's slow and not meant to carry an entire floor's worth of people in a hurry.

How is the elevator even working since the power cut out?

"You go on ahead. I'll be right behind you."

Wisdom dictates staying in the less hectic office versus becoming trampling fodder in the hall, except our supervisor pokes his head in the room, a harried expression on his craggy face.

"Everyone evacuate. A water main blew, and it's screwing with our pipes. We need to get out."

"You don't have to tell me twice." Shawna hustles out the door behind Harold.

"Okay, guess I'm wading into the melee," I mutter to myself.

The din in the hall has lessened, but there are still stragglers waiting for the elevator.

Using an electric death box in the middle of a water emergency seems like a scene from *Final Destination* waiting to happen, so I bypass the small crowd and head toward the stairs.

The sound of rushing water becomes louder during my careful descent to safety. It's apparent that a whole bunch of ancient City Hall pipes decided to take a page from the water main and burst open.

Trickling water slicks down the walls to gleam on the floor, and my steps grow reluctant, since my sensible low-heeled pumps don't have the best traction.

And I'm not about to traipse barefoot through bacteria-filled floodwater.

Once I reach the last stair on the ground floor, there's at least a foot of water between me and the exit, and black and yellow uniforms dot the halls as firemen usher employees out the main entrance.

How the hell did it get this high already?

As I contemplate my options—*newsflash, I have none*—one firefighter breaks from his position a few feet down the hall and trudges my way.

One very familiar firefighter.

"Beckett! It's you!" *Gee, can I be any more embarrassing?*

Because Beckett, the town's resident bad boy, is fucking hot.

So hot that the connection between my mind and tongue is suddenly broken.

Suspenders climb over his broad shoulders and clip to oversized pants, while his short-sleeved Suitor's Crossing Fire Department shirt is anything *but* oversized. It conforms to his firm muscles like he's dressed for a fireman calendar rather than saving women from watery disasters.

"It's me," he says, a quizzical half-grin lifting his lips. "I'm sorry, but do I know you?"

The answer is *yes*.

Yes, I can be more embarrassing.

This man has no idea who the hell I am, and I'm greeting him like a long-lost friend. *Kill me now.* Drown me in dirty pipe water and end my suffering.

"I live across from the firehouse."

Face, meet Palm. Because *that* doesn't sound creepy at all.

He stares at me like I've grown two heads... or like he's acquired another stalker. It's no secret how popular Beckett Caldwell is among the women of Suitor's Crossing. He's probably got his fair share of clingers and wannabe baby mamas.

Sadly, you will probably find my name on that list, too.

"I heard a lot of your names when you ran drills outside. Collin, Grady, Isla..." *Big Billy with the two left feet*, my scrambled brain jokes. "Plus, you live with Ranger, right? Caroline is one of my best friends, so I'm at the Reaper's Wolves MC clubhouse a lot and have seen you with him."

Good god, why am I still rambling? Shut up already!

If he didn't think I was a stalker before, he definitely does now, which means I should probably keep my friendship with his sister, Kennedy, to myself, too.

"Not that I track when you're at the clubhouse. It's just that I'm there, and you're sometimes there..." A forced laugh that sounds suspiciously close to hysteria erupts before my lips seal in a concrete line.

No more talking.

No more, Elizabeth Anne Dayton!

The fire of humiliation burns across my skin as Beckett's gaze widens and his *oh-so-kissable* mouth twitches.

Probably trying not to gape in shock at how unhinged I sound.

Just what every girl dreams of when being rescued by her secret crush.

Face, meet Palm... Again.

CHAPTER TWO

BECKETT CALDWELL

She's cute.

A complete and utter stranger, but cute.

And fire-engine red from the tips of her exposed ears down to her chest and crossed arms.

Good thing red is my favorite color.

"Why don't we start with your name, while I get you safely outside?" I ask with a raised brow once she stops nervously rambling.

Another pretty blush stains her cheeks, and she nods, allowing me to wrap one arm around her back and the other beneath her knees.

With a slight heft to secure her against my chest, I turn to wade back through one of the more interesting ways I've started a Monday morning—a busted water main and a woman with an adorable penchant for babbling in my arms.

"So..." I lightly bounce my arm along her back, and the movement causes a chain reaction from her jiggling tits straight to my cock. Dragging my eyes upward, I focus on not tripping on anything hiding in the water, clear my throat, and ask again, "What's your name, beautiful?"

"Oh, um... Elizabeth. *Beth*."

"And you're friends with the Reaper's Wolves MC women?"

"And your sister." She slams her mouth shut as if she shouldn't have voiced that connection, too.

In such a small town, and with so many mutual friends, I'm surprised we haven't officially met before.

I voice my thoughts, sidestepping a floating trash bin.

She manages a shrug as her grip around my neck tightens. "I haven't lived in Suitor's Crossing long... *Fuck*!" A spray of water explodes from the wall to our left to nail both of us in the face.

"Shit!" I shout and spin to take the brunt of the impact, although we're both coughing water out of our mouths.

It's no secret that City Hall is old. Hell, a lot of the original buildings on Main Street are. But the pipes shouldn't be so rickety as to pop like cans of biscuits straight out of the fucking wall.

My booted feet quicken their pace until solid ground greets me instead of splashes of water and squishy carpet.

The City Hall entry steps are dark from moisture, but at least they're not slick, and we're no longer in danger of getting blasted from another rogue pipe.

"Are you okay?" I carefully lower Beth to the grass a slight distance from the crowd of people staring at the flooded building.

The police have cordoned off the street on three sides of the structure, and a line of traffic clogs the fourth side.

It's going to be a bitch for anyone to leave with their car. Street parking is blocked either by other vehicles or caution tape—not to mention the small lake the burst water main created.

Beth dries her cheeks with the bottom of her cardigan. "Yeah, I'm fine. Thank you for rescuing me."

"It was my pleasure." A jolt of bewilderment catches me off-guard.

It *was* a pleasure holding her in my arms.

Listening to her awkwardly explain knowing who I am.

She's not the first woman I've saved on the job, and she won't be the last, yet I'm lingering by her side, remembering the feel of her in my arms when I should get back to work.

I've dealt with transference in the past. When someone I rescued attached romantic feelings to me because of the heroic act.

But this is the first time the opposite has happened.

Bullshit.

Ridding myself of the ridiculous notion—this is plain-old attraction, not the beginning of a romantic attachment, or fucking *heart sparks*—I decide it's time to leave before I do something stupid like ask for her number.

I don't date locally.

Not anymore.

My family already makes fun of the *bad boy* reputation I earned in high school that then followed me into adulthood. I'm not about to add to the lore by fucking one of Kennedy's friends.

Hell. No.

Raising a hand in farewell, I mutter, "See you around," then stalk back to what should be my primary focus—a flooded City Hall.

Not a cute, curvy stranger.

"Was that our neighbor I saw you with?" Grady asks upon my approach a few minutes later. We started at the firehouse around the same time and naturally gravitated toward each other, forming an easy friendship.

"Our neighbor? You know Beth?"

Grady smirks. "A pretty girl lives across the street from where we eat, sleep, and work dozens of hours a week? Yeah, I noticed her, though I don't *know* her... yet." He slaps the back of my shoulder with a confident wink.

Usually, Grady and I get along fine. We've been each other's wingman too many times to count whenever I'm looking for a little fun and female companionship in Seattle. But, for some reason, his cavalier attitude about Beth grates on my nerves.

"Keep it that way," I grunt, watching as more City Hall employees are hustled out of the building.

"I know you have a rule about not dating anyone local, but I don't."

"You're free to date whoever you want except for Beth. She's off-limits." I don't know why I'm pushing this. Didn't I already decide that this is a perfectly normal physical attraction, and not something more?

Why should I care who Beth dates?

Why should I care if the man she allows to touch all those soft curves is one of my closest friends?

Grady tilts his head, confusion wrinkling around his eyes. "You want her? That's not like you."

"She's friends with my sister," I say by way of explanation. "She's too close to home."

"Right..." Grady drawls. "But *she* isn't your actual sister." We're silent for a moment, then he shrugs nonchalantly and raises his hands. "Whatever, no hot neighbor for me. Ready to get back to work?"

Our captain is waving us over, and I exhale in relief, nodding as we walk his way. Anything to distract me from the uncomfortable conversation.

And from thoughts of Beth, our *hot neighbor*.

CHAPTER THREE

BETH

Cream pages flip in a mesmerizing display—a shot of calming serotonin straight to my brain. Words blur, and the whisper of a breeze brushes the back of my hand as I absentmindedly start the process over again. Too in my head to focus on the conversation around me.

Another book club meeting.

Another night pretending not to envy my friends.

I don't begrudge their happiness, but is it too much to ask for some of it to come my way?

They've found love in Suitor's Crossing.

All I've gained after moving here a year ago is ten pounds.

And an embarrassing memory that confirms I might be single forever.

God, why did I have to freak out on Beckett? Why couldn't I be cool or witty or literally a thousand other things besides neurotic?

I flip the book in my hands over again and watch three hundred pages of a couple falling in love condense into hazy smudges.

"Are you okay?" Faith leans over to check on me.

"Yeah, I'm good," I lie. What other choice do I have? I can't admit to a mini pity party during one of the best nights of the week for me.

Hanging out at the Reaper's Wolves MC compound with Caroline, Faith, Kat, Amelie, and Lindy is always fun, and we just started a new hockey romance series. I should be excited to chat about the hot goalie and his taboo relationship with the coach's daughter, yet here I am.

Wallowing in my lack of romantic prospects.

For a town known for bringing soulmates, or *heart sparks*, together, Suitor's Crossing has really let me down so far.

Maybe I should walk across that infamous bridge—the town's version of Cupid—for the hundredth time.

Maybe Walk #100 will be my lucky number.

"Are you sure? It's been an eventful week for you since that water main burst."

Overhearing us, Caroline glances over. "How are you dealing with that? City Hall is shut down for who knows how long, and don't you have fall events to plan?"

"Losing the office hasn't been an issue. I don't mind working from home. The problem is the Chili Cook-Off fundraiser on Saturday. We had everything ready to go, and now we're scrambling to figure something else out, since it was supposed to take place in front of City Hall. The pipes and road won't be fixed in the next two days because they're dealing with the utility lines, too. It's just a mess."

I rub my forehead as another headache threatens to form.

The stress of having months of planning literally washed down the drain and needing to start from scratch to cram all that work into mere days is wreaking havoc with my brain. And appetite. And sleep.

Basically, this week has sucked.

The only bright spot was being held those few moments in Beckett's strong arms, and even that memory is tainted by my humiliating word vomit.

"I'm sure you could move the event to another section of Main Street," Lindy offers, "but aren't you friends with Kennedy Caldwell? Didn't the two of you work together on an event in the past? Maybe Hearthstone Lodge has an open space where you can hold the Cook-Off. They are used to hosting all sorts of things, so it might be easy to transition locations."

"That's a good idea," I say, my fingers drifting to massage my temple. "Maybe I'll text Kennedy and see what she thinks. In the meantime, which player do you think the next book will be about?"

The girls accept the subject change and argue over their favorite side character, while I rest my head on the back of the couch, grateful to not be the center of attention anymore.

I should have skipped tonight's book club.

Vegging out in my bed wrapped in a cocoon of blankets sounds heavenly right about now.

Maybe I can bow out early.

Commotion at the compound entrance draws my eye when Fox and Ranger enter the communal living space. Our book club doesn't always meet in the main MC hang out, but sometimes it's nice to spread out on the huge couches rather than staying cozy in the cabin Caroline shares with Snow, the MC President.

A breath of relief slowly slides from my lips as I notice Ranger and Fox are alone and not accompanied by Ranger's roommate,

Beckett. The man probably already thinks I'm a stalker. He doesn't need to see me lounging in the MC living room like I'm waiting for him to show up.

Even if I have a perfectly logical excuse to be here.

Even though I've seen him several times in the past during book club, when he appeared with Ranger and a couple other MC guys.

Ugh! Closing my eyes, I will myself to stop obsessing over Beckett.

It doesn't work; it never does.

But a girl can try.

CHAPTER FOUR

BECKETT

The Suitor's Crossing Senior Center is busier than The Ole Aces on a Friday night, and that's saying something since it's a Thursday afternoon.

Pink, purple, and silver-haired ladies swing their artificial hips around the center's dance floor, while men in orthopedic shoes shuffle at their sides to a lively polka number.

Gramps bends to whisper something into his partner Lucille's ear, and they both laugh as they circle the floor.

Seeing his happiness makes me smile, while I search the edges of the room for my younger brother, Griffen. He's our grandpa's caretaker and never far from his side, though Gramps is more independent than I think Griffen gives him credit for.

Finding my brother saddled in a chair too small for his giant frame, I head in his direction.

"Hey, man." I raise a fist to bump his in greeting before taking a seat next to him.

"What are you doing here?" he asks.

"Kennedy called. Guess the lodge will be hosting the Chili Cook-Off this weekend, and I'm here to recruit you for set-up tonight. Her schedule is packed tomorrow, so this is the only evening she has free time before Saturday morning."

Griffen grunts and shrugs his massive shoulders. Though he's the youngest of my brothers, he's the biggest, and the Caldwell men aren't exactly slouches in the size department.

"Sure, just let me know what time. This is all Gramps has planned today." He motions toward the dance floor. Gramps and Lucille have found new partners with the changing of the song.

"What about you? You know you don't have to stay here monitoring his every step. You can have your own life."

"I'm good," he says, and I shake my head at his stubbornness.

It's not that he's anti-social, but Griffen is on the shyer, more introverted side of our family. He and our sister Kennedy are two peas in a pod when it comes to that sort of thing.

"*You're good,*" I murmur under my breath. He's a lone wolf is what he is. "You need some fun. To get laid. Hell, you act like a member of the senior center despite being forty-fucking-years too young."

My gaze travels over the group of geriatrics my brother has chosen as his companions until a misplaced woman—a *young* woman with her eyes stuck on Griffen—stops my perusal.

"What about her? She seems interested." I discreetly gesture to the girl.

Her strawberry blonde hair is braided into a crown around her head, and she seems to be recreating the style on the lady seated in front of her.

"Heidi?" Griffen stiffens beside me. A flush rises on his cheeks, and I grin.

"Yeah, *Heidi*. Looks like you're interested, too, baby brother." My elbow playfully nudges him as I surreptitiously glance between Heidi and Griffen, amused by the sudden tension in the air.

Sexual tension.

At least, that's what I'm chalking it up to, hopeful for my boulder of a little brother.

"We've barely spoken to each other," he says, like that explains why he's blushing at the mention of her name.

"Doesn't matter. She keeps stealing peeks at you. Go over there and ask her out."

"Just because you flirt with every woman in your vicinity, and have left a string of sexual conquests behind you, that doesn't mean I want the same thing."

"What the hell? I'm trying to help you. You make me sound like an asshole." My teeth grind together at his description of my romantic past. I haven't been a saint, but damn, it's not like I lead women on.

They know the score.

They want a hot night with a firefighter? I give it to them. No strings attached.

"Sorry." Griffen sighs. "I'm just not like you. That's all I'm saying."

I bump his knee with mine. "Thank fuck. There's only room for one bad boy Caldwell in this town," I joke. "But seriously, if you're not interested in Heidi, that's cool. Just... Think about it. Think about your life outside of Gramps. You deserve something for yourself."

He grimaces but nods, and I know that's the best I can expect from Griffen on the subject.

CHAPTER FIVE

BETH

Damn this week, and damn this fucking headache that's trying to kill me.

Cursing is supposed to alter your perception of pain. Make it seem less than agonizing.

A lot of good it's done me so far.

Changing tactics, my inner tirade transforms into a polite plea for relief as another sharp pain pierces my temple.

Kennedy relieved a lot of my stress by agreeing to host the Chili Cook-Off at Hearthstone.

She even volunteered to find extra people to help me set up everything, since most of the lodge staff were busy with another event, yet these damn headaches keep plaguing me.

No matter what I do.

Tons of water and electrolyte-filled Gatorade have been sloshing around in my stomach. My only reward? Numerous visits to the bathroom to pee and a slight feeling of nausea.

I've worn my hair down—no efficient ponytail to tug on my sensitive scalp, not even a bobby pin to hold my hair back from my face.

And nothing.

All of my usual go-tos for defeating headaches have failed. Including hot showers, classical music, and the weird magical powers of drinking nasty Coke soda.

Which means it's time to break out the ibuprofen and acetaminophen.

Something I avoid at all costs because I hate swallowing pills.

My brain shuts down, and the pill sits on my tongue, slowly dissolving into a gross flavor that makes me want to gag, because it takes me so long to trick my mind into swallowing.

I don't know why I struggle so much, but it's been a problem since I was a kid.

I remember the very first time my mom offered me a Tylenol when I was twelve years old and got my period. It took so long to swallow that I ended up crying out of embarrassment and irrational fear.

Oh, yeah, and don't forget the painful cramps and headache!

"Suck it up, buttercup," I scold myself and remove the travel-sized pill organizer from my purse. It holds my emergency stash of ibuprofen, acetaminophen, and an antihistamine for when allergies are kicking my butt.

Popping two pills in my mouth, I scream in my head, *Swallow!*, praying the firm directive will force my body to follow the command.

"Nice pep talk," someone says from behind me.

You've got to be kidding me.

My shoulders slump as my eyes flutter shut in defeat. I do *not* need a witness to my illogical response to swallowing pills. Especially not *this* witness.

Of the sexy firefighter variety.

What's he doing here?

It's his family's lodge, but still... It's not like he lives or works here. Shouldn't he be at the firehouse across town?

The pills slide under my tongue as I garble, "Hey, Beckett."

"Are you alright?" He steps in front of me, and I frantically nod, sipping at the water bottle in my hand.

I shake my pill organizer in explanation of my nonverbal response and grit my teeth.

Swallow!

Swallow, or else!

Finally, the medicine works its way down my throat—*score one for threats*—and I chug the water to get rid of the awful taste in my mouth.

"I'm fine. Just a minor headache."

"Are you sure? Seems more than that."

I drag a bright smile to the forefront, attempting to mask my discomfort. "What? No. You caught me off guard. I hate swallowing pills, and you appeared right as I took them, and—"

My lips smack together as I cut off my rambling.

What the hell is wrong with me when it comes to this man?

For some reason, my composure flies out the window, and I can't keep my mouth shut. It's weird and out of character because I'm usually overthinking and overly cautious with my words.

Beckett obliterates that filter when he should be the one who causes me to clam up even tighter.

Because I want to impress him.

I want him to like me.

I inwardly groan at feeling like a middle schooler with their first crush.

"They make powdered packets of ibuprofen and acetaminophen. Other meds, too. Have you tried that?" he asks, concern dotting his expression.

No.

No, I have not.

Because I didn't know that was A. Fucking. Thing!

I really should research more.

"Nope, but I'll look into it. Are you here to help prepare for the fundraiser?" Switching subjects seems best if I want to hang on to a shred of my dignity.

You know, the teeny scrap that is left.

"Yeah, Kennedy asked us." He must be referring to his brothers—the rest of the Caldwell siblings, who I haven't seen yet, but I'm guessing are filling the banquet room with tables and chairs. "Here, let me help you while we're waiting for the pain meds to kick in."

Beckett eases closer, his large palms moving to either side of my head, before the confident massage of fingertips against my throbbing temples sends a river of goosebumps over my skin.

"Um... You don't have to do t-that," I stutter, frozen in place under his firm but careful ministrations.

This close, the silver of his eyes is a bullet straight to my racing heart, and it's a good thing I'm not a fucking werewolf because I'd be dead on the floor.

Death by a handsome fireman.

What a way to go...

Why does he affect me so strongly?

Beckett has an identical twin.

Ezra has the same steel gray eyes and black hair, though he's more polished. His hair styled rather than left shaggy like Beckett's.

More likely to be found in a suit than tees. He's more serious, and by all accounts, we share a lot of similar personality traits.

But he's not the one I want.

I mean he's taken now by Lauren, but even when he was single, he's never been the Caldwell twin I've been drawn to.

It's always been Beckett.

From the first time I saw him across the street hauling hoses across the firehouse's front lawn during a training exercise. Then again, when he'd surprised me by appearing at the Reaper's Wolves MC clubhouse with Ranger during a book club meeting.

"Actually, I do. It's part of my job description as a first responder: always provide whatever aid is necessary." He winks, and a flicker of excitement wings to life in my belly.

Is he flirting with me?

Is he not totally scared off by my nervous chatter and slightly stalkerish admissions?

"This seems excessive, though. Do you always go so far above and beyond your call of duty?"

"When it comes to you, I'm beginning to think there's nothing I wouldn't do."

The sharp intake of my breath is the only sound in the hall after his confession.

I think it surprised him, too, based on the stiffening around his jaw. The jolt of his fingers on my skin.

Beckett clears his throat then drops his hold on me, retreating several feet away like I'm suddenly infected with cooties.

"Hopefully, that helped some. I should return to the banquet room." He jerks a thumb down the hall. The sound of voices and the clanging of chairs and tables being unfolded reverberates in the air. "See you in there."

"Yeah... See you."

I give him a head start, not wanting to shadow his footsteps so quickly, despite going to the same place.

He's already trying to escape whatever this moment was. I don't need to make it even more awkward.

The back of my head lightly knocks against the wall where I lean for support.

Did I really think he was flirting?

What a fucking joke...

CHAPTER SIX

BECKETT

"Earth to Beckett! Anyone home?" My twin brother calls my name from across the six-foot folding table we're adding to the line of tables against the north wall.

According to Kennedy and Beth, this is where the fundraiser contestants will set up their cooking stations.

"I'm right here. No need to shout."

Ezra snickers and moves to grab the next folded table. "Then consider responding the first time I say your name."

"Whatever," I mumble with little heat.

I'm not in the mood to banter with my brother. I'm too distracted by the curvy woman currently smoothing out a wrinkle in the tablecloth she is positioning on a table further down the line from us.

Her round ass wiggles as she bends further, the back of her shirt riding up to reveal a sliver of soft, pale skin, and my mouth goes dry at the sight.

What the fuck?

This isn't Victorian England.

One smooth strip of a woman's back shouldn't make my heart pound or my cock thicken in anticipation.

Anticipation for *what*, I'd rather not hazard a guess.

"Something going on there?" Ezra asks as he shuffles over to my side.

"What? Where?" *Playing dumb.* Always the best strategy when you want to avoid answering uncomfortable questions. Especially from family.

Ezra ignores my poor attempt at evasion. "You know what. That woman over there. Eliza? Lizzie?"

"Beth," I correct him automatically, before immediately regretting it once I realize he was playing me. Pretending not to remember her name to force my hand.

"Yeah, *Beth*... Kennedy's friend." There's a wealth of meaning in those two little words.

Because we don't fuck our sister's friends.

Granted, the rule is moot for Soren and Ezra since they've already fallen in love with their own women, but it still stands for me and Griffen.

Especially for me.

Because I don't do drama.

I don't date within the Suitor's Crossing town limits.

Yet I'm contemplating breaking all of those rules with Beth.

She's gotten under my skin during our brief interactions. Hell, I almost kissed her in the hall after spouting that sappy shit about 'nothing I wouldn't do' for her.

Once my brain caught up to what my reckless mouth was saying, I took control of that shit and booked it out of there.

"It's about time you got here!" Kennedy's voice rings out from across the room, and I look up to see who she's talking to.

Grady and a few guys from third-shift saunter through the doorway. My sister must have roped them into helping, too, since the fundraiser is for the firehouse.

Grady waves in greeting but continues walking to where Beth is straightening another tablecloth. His chin dips, and I can tell he's checking out her ass.

My fists clench around the metal table in my hand. Sweat makes my hold slippery, and it crashes to the floor with an ear-piercing clatter.

Everyone stares before returning to what they were doing.

Everyone except for me.

Because I'm too focused on watching Grady sidle up to Beth.

"She may be Kennedy's friend, but we're adults now. If you want her, you shouldn't let her connection to our sister stop you, especially if you don't want Grady snatching her for himself." Ezra picks up the fallen table with a pointed stare at the couple.

They're not a couple.

Fuck, I don't know what's wrong with me.

I don't get jealous or possessive over women. Grady chatting up Beth shouldn't annoy me, even if I did warn him away from her.

Because he was right.

Beth isn't my sister.

He doesn't have a rule about dating locals. I'm the one with the issues, not him.

So, why shouldn't he flirt with her?

Because she's mine.

The immediate feral response punches me in the gut. It's illogical. The claim of a Neanderthal, which I've never been accused of being.

Sure, I've got the bad boy reputation, but I'm a *good* man. I treat women with respect and don't view them as objects to own.

But I can't shake this feeling that Beth belongs to me.

After laughing at something Grady says, she pats his arm then exits the room. Probably to grab more supplies from the lodge's storage closet. We keep all sorts of decorations, furniture, and whatever other crap Hearthstone has accumulated over the years in there.

One kiss, I reason.

One kiss, that's it.

Maybe the outlet will rid me of this obsession for Beth, because right now, she's a mystery.

A beautiful, curvy mystery.

I know we run in the same social circles, despite never meeting before this week, and I know she works at City Hall. That she lives across from the fire station.

Three basic things that barely scratch the surface of a person, yet I'm beguiled enough to contemplate throwing caution to the wind and breaking all my rules for her.

To hell with it.

My determined stride shoots me past contemplation and headfirst into action.

I've already decided to steal one small piece of Beth for myself.

One fucking kiss.

CHAPTER SEVEN

BETH

Something must be in the air this week.

I don't run into a lot of single attractive guys in town.

Men in my orbit are usually in a relationship or not my type. The Reaper's Wolves MC members don't count since they're technically on the edge of town, and I hang out where they live. *They* don't come to *me*.

Unlike Beckett.

Or Grady.

When the tall, blonde-haired firefighter skipped getting an assignment from Kennedy like his buddies or joining Beckett and Ezra on the other side of the room, my breath stuttered to a halt.

He didn't cause me to get all jittery like Beckett, but Grady is still attractive. And guys don't approach me as easily as they do someone like Ezra's partner, Lauren, or Soren's girl, Diana.

Yet twice this week, I've had sexy men thrown my way.

Something must be in the air...

Or maybe heart sparks *are finally doing their fucking job and finding me love?*

"Keep smoothing out the wrinkles. I'm going to grab more tablecloths. Be right back," I tell Grady, hightailing it out of the banquet room for a breather.

A short-lived one.

Because Beckett follows me into the hall. His familiar cologne tickles my nose right before his warm hand tugs on mine from behind.

"Beth, wait up."

Refusing to stop and embarrass myself again, I keep walking, quickening my pace.

Beckett's grip on me remains steady. The rough texture of his palm is evidence of his hands-on job, and I can't resist gently swiping a thumb over a callus.

No! Bad Beth!

"Beth, please. Stop." Exasperation coats his tone, along with a note of... desperation?

Dream on, girl.

Beckett isn't desperate for me. He probably wants—well, I'm not sure what he could possibly want to say, but it's probably not along the lines of *Beth, you're the most amazing woman in the world. Please be mine for all eternity.*

Picturing bad boy Beckett resorting to over-the-top declarations of love almost makes me snort in laughter.

"*Elizabeth.*"

My full name shouldn't sound so hot coming from him. I'm a grown-ass woman, not a child who needs scolding, but a shudder of arousal drips between my thighs anyway.

"For chrissakes!" He uses his strength to halt my forward progress and swings me around until my back is against the wall. "You shouldn't run from me," he reprimands.

His body heat seeps through my blouse as his broad chest brushes my nipples.

"I-I wasn't running."

"You didn't stop."

I don't have an excuse for that. It's not like I can lie about hearing him. He was two freaking feet away. And had possession of my hand.

Gathering my wits, I straighten my spine, ignoring the fact that he still towers over me, even when I'm standing at my full height. "Did you need something? I'm headed to the supply closet, so I can—"

"The only thing I need is you," he rasps then urges me closer to meet his slightly parted lips.

What. The. Fuck.

I gasp in shock, a sharp inhale that burns in my chest, before I slowly relax in Beckett's possessive embrace.

His tongue sweeps forward in a bold move. Controlling the kiss. Controlling me with confident hands as he pins my arms to my sides.

The flush of my full curves trapped between Beckett's hard muscles and a stone wall should feel suffocating. Claustrophobic. Instead, I feel cozy. Safe. Surrounded by his spicy scent and addictive warmth.

He breaks away for a second, and my lips are left bereft. I keep my lashes firmly shut to pretend like I can stay in this fantasy forever. Then there's a low murmur. "Come home with me tonight."

Wait, what? My eyes spring open. *Did... Did he just...?*

"Um... why?" *And the award for World's Dumbest Question goes to Beth Dayton!*

But seriously, what do you expect? No one has ever propositioned me for sex before. Especially no one like Beckett freaking Caldwell. All dangerous smiles and protective instincts. Even if a man *did* ask me for sex, I'm not that kind of girl.

I'm too cautious to sleep with a stranger, or a *kinda* stranger who I've only talked to a handful of times.

I don't do flings.

I don't do one-night-stands.

But I like Beckett.

He's my secret crush.

And that's the problem.

I shouldn't spend time with him *in his bed* when I already have feelings. Because knowing what it feels like to be the center of Beckett's attention is a recipe for disaster.

"Why should you come home with me?" A wolfish grin bares his white teeth. "Because I want you to. Because I can't get you out of my head." He nips at my bottom lip before licking the sting away. "I can't explain it, baby, but I need more. I think we both do, and a night of hot sex sounds just about right."

Not exactly the romantic declaration I imagined, but it's honest.

"Beth?" My name is a question on his tongue, and despite my cautious nature, and all the warnings going off in my head, my chin dips in agreement.

This man really does scramble everything I've ever known about myself.

"Yes, I'll come home with you. We have maybe an hour left here before I can leave, though."

Beckett nods in understanding and lets me go.

The wide grin lighting up his face almost makes me think that the pain that will come once we're over will be worth it.

Almost.

CHAPTER EIGHT

BETH

When we arrive at Beckett's home, I'm surprised to learn that instead of a bachelor pad in one of the apartment complexes in town, he lives in a two-story Craftsman.

"Wow," I say as he parks in the two-car garage. "This is a lot of house."

"Don't worry, it's not all for me. My best friend, Ranger, and I share the place. You might have met him."

Right.

For a second, the wildness of what I'm doing eclipsed the part of my brain that knew he and Ranger were roommates.

"I'm surprised an MC guy lives off the compound."

"He's not the only one." Beckett rounds the vehicle to open my door. "Ranger and I were roommates in college. After he got out of the military and..." He trails off and shakes his head like he shouldn't say something. "Moved to Suitor's Crossing, it wasn't that big of a leap for us to rent something together. He commandeered the basement. I've got the upstairs, and we share the first-floor kitchen and living areas. It's a good compromise. We both have our own spaces."

"It sounds like a dream."

If most of my friends weren't in serious relationships, I'd suggest we share a large home like this.

Unfortunately, Kat and I are the only single girls left from our original book club group, and Kat still lives in Everton, where we all resided before the Great Migration to Suitor's Crossing.

Beckett punches in a security code and unlocks a door that opens into a kitchen full of shadows.

"Is Ranger here?" I ask, a little uncomfortable with the idea of him hearing us together.

Though, he is probably used to Beckett bringing women home.

Don't think about that!

I shake the thought off as I attempt to hype myself up and remember why I'm here.

I'm going to have sex with Beckett Caldwell.

Me, not-so-cautious-now Beth.

Beckett shakes his head and flips on a light. "No, he's out on club business. Which means I've got you all to myself."

Oozing confidence, Beckett whisks me upstairs to his bedroom, which better fits my idea of a bachelor pad.

Chrome details.

Sparse knickknacks.

Function over form.

His arms wrap around my waist, silver eyes studying my expression as I look around the room. It's a decent size with a huge king bed centered on one wall.

"Are you sure you're okay with this? You can change your mind at any time." Beckett's quiet voice interrupts my obvious inspection.

"I want this. Promise." I lift up to press my mouth to his and silence the nagging worries in the back of my mind.

Because I *do* want this.

It's only fear of the future that has my stomach tied in knots.

Worry for when he moves on to someone else.

Because this is Beckett Caldwell we're talking about.

The Suitor's Crossing bad boy.

He literally leaves town for hook-ups because they're so prolific.

Which reminds me.

Rearing back, I quickly ask, "Healthwise... I'm good. What about you?"

"Tested regularly. We're in the clear."

I release a breath of relief before Beckett retakes control of the kiss and backs me into his bed.

We flop down onto the mattress in a chaotic heap.

Hands, tongues, teeth.

His palm slides expertly underneath my shirt to unhook my bra, and soon I'm naked from the waist up. The man has had some serious practice undressing a woman.

Stop thinking about his past.

"Goddamn, you're pretty," he whispers in awe, and a bit of my self-consciousness fades away.

"Your turn." I tug on his shirt with trembling fingers.

Unlike me, Beckett has abs for days. It's evident how hard he works to remain in shape for his job.

"Wow," I say dumbly. My fingertips trace the deep indentations of his muscular stomach, drifting over the 'V' lines leading to his groin.

"Like what you see, baby?" he teases, thrusting into my tentative grip around his boxer-brief-covered dick.

Licking my lips, I nod, words escaping me.

"Me, too." Beckett groans, and his fingers toy with the button of my jeans, waiting for my silent consent.

I give it to him with one quick nod.

There's the rasp of the zipper then cool air wafts over my bare hips and thighs. The man is dragging my panties off with my jeans, and a wave of nervous anticipation crashes in my veins.

"Oh my God," I gasp after the first confident press of Beckett's thumb on my clit.

"This is only the beginning."

He kisses down my collarbone and nips at my nipples with his teeth before licking the sting away. Before continuing his southern trajectory.

He nudges my thighs further apart, one hand bracing on the inside of my thigh to hold me open for his perusal. His silver gaze a physical caress over my skin.

"Beckett," I plead, one part self-conscious, the other, needing him to stop staring and start *doing*.

"What do you need? My tongue inside this pretty cunt?" He demonstrates with a firm thrust of the flexible muscle through my clenching walls, and I whimper in response.

"Or do you need it wrapped around your clit?" Beckett strikes again. This time curling his tongue around the sensitive bud atop my sex.

"What do you need, Beth?" he repeats.

I seriously hope he doesn't need me to answer that, because it's all I can do not to black out from the pleasure of his fingers and mouth manipulating my aching flesh.

"Whatever you want, I need whatever you want to give me. *Please."*

"So accommodating," he rumbles. "Such a good girl."

Then, his wicked grin disappears in the shadow of my thighs. His hot tongue licking where no man has ever been before.

I arch into his ravenous mouth, my fingers scrambling for purchase on his shoulders, then his scalp, scratching and pulling, urging him on.

I don't know if it pains him, or if it does, if he *likes* it.

Because Beckett just grunts and redoubles his efforts, devouring my pussy like a hungry bear diving into a pot of honey.

His beard scrapes; his lips soothe.

And he eats, eats, *eats*, until I come on a scream, my body quaking in pleasure from his rough feasting.

"You're fucking delicious, baby." Beckett rises to his knees with a cocky smirk.

The evidence of my arousal gleams on his mouth, and another shudder wracks my limbs when he licks his lips with a hum of approval.

"You feel incredible wrapped around my tongue, but I know you'll feel even better snug around my dick."

He reaches over to the drawer of his nightstand and pulls out a condom.

I watch in fascination as the thin rubber drags down his thick cock. Somewhere along the line, he lost his boxer briefs, allowing me free access to the sight of his heavy dick and balls hanging between his legs.

I can't tear my attention away from the mesmerizing display of male virility.

Until the broad head of his cock nudges at my entrance.

My clouded gaze meets his, and once again he waits for my permission to continue.

"Please." One word, but it's all he needs to thrust forward.

So big and long that he bumps against my cervix.

"Beckett!"

I've heard stories about it being painful when a man goes that deep, but then I've also seen accounts about cervical orgasms being more powerful than clitoral ones.

Since I'm not in pain, I pray I'm one of those lucky women who experiences the latter.

Could I really be so lucky?

It seems I'm already using my fair share by spending the night beneath Beckett's rock-hard body.

"Thats right, Beth. Scream my name. Let my neighbors hear how well you take my cock." He retreats, then slides forward again.

In.

Out.

Slowly quickening his pace until the headboard bangs against the wall, and I slide up the bed.

Until every thick vein and hard ridge of his cock strokes each tingling inch of my pussy. The massive head battering deep.

We're both sweating. Breathing hard. Animalistic sounds rumbling between us.

Sex with Beckett is dirty and hot, slick with our desire, and I can't get enough.

"Come for me, Beth. Come for me, baby."

I'm powerless to deny him.

My mouth opens on a silent shout as the strongest orgasm I've ever had rends me in two, and with a roar of his own, Beckett isn't far behind me.

Just before I pass out from the pleasure, I send up a desperate prayer.

Please don't let this be all I ever get of this man.

I don't think I'll be able to survive it.

CHAPTER NINE

BECKETT

The next morning, I wake up to a cold and empty bed.

"Beth?" I ask the unusually quiet room after a night of breathy moans and sweet whimpers.

Having Beth in my bed, cuddled into me, was... different.

Amazing.

Totally addictive.

The only issue is that she's not still here. Not snuggled into my side like a warm, purring kitten.

Did she leave already?

Did she sneak out without saying goodbye?

In seconds, I've disentangled myself from the cluster of blankets and swung open the bedroom door, prepared to find my missing girl.

Sweatpants hang from my hips, my hair is askew, and my socked feet slip on the floor as I race downstairs to the main level.

Fuck, I didn't even take my socks off last night?

It's not lost on me how atypical my behavior has become.

I've never brought a woman home with me. I don't spend the night either. We fuck then go our separate ways.

And I remember to take off all my damn clothes.

But Beth is unique.

She's more than a fling.

Something I feared yesterday when I thought a kiss would get her out of my system.

Because that particular notion was swiftly dispelled the moment our lips touched. I knew then and there that I craved more.

Which is why I invited her back to my place.

Except now she is gone without a trace.

Ranger lazes in the living room on his phone when he sees what must be my crazy-eyed look. His feet are propped on a leather ottoman while old cartoons play on the TV, reminding me of a conversation I had with my family about how classic animated shows calmed me. Ranger and I both discovered their relaxing effects in college.

He smirks then jerks a thumb to the left. "She's in the kitchen."

I didn't even have to say a word for him to know who I was searching for.

Probably because he'd feel the same way if it were Georgia who disappeared on him.

She's the manager of Club Wolf 2.0—not its official name—and he's been spending a lot of time with her since the original Club Wolf burned down. She also happens to be a Reaper's Wolves MC member's sister.

Grim will blow a gasket when he finds out one of his MC brothers has a thing for his little sister.

Though considering the other secret Ranger is hiding, maybe that'll be the least of his worries...

Putting Ranger and his potential problems out of my head, I hurry into the kitchen, my pace stalling once Beth comes into view. She's seated at the center island eating a bowl of cereal.

"Hey, you disappeared." *No shit, Sherlock.* What a stupid way to say *good morning.*

"My stomach wouldn't shut up, so I figured I'd eat something before going home to finish last-minute details for tomorrow's cook-off." Her body tenses, and a frown tugs at her lush mouth. "I hope that's okay. That I'm still here."

"Of course." I drop a kiss to the top of her head. "Do you have to be home by a certain time?"

The clock on the oven shows that it's just after 8:00 A.M.

"My Teams chat should show I'm *available*—" Her fingers make little air quotes—"by 9:00, so we've got plenty of time if you need to shower or eat breakfast or whatever. I don't want to disrupt your normal routine."

"Don't worry about it. My next shift isn't until Monday, so my day is flexible."

After grabbing a bowl and spoon, I join her at the island. Our knees brush under the marble overhang, and a zing of electricity emanates from the connection.

My theory about getting Beth out of my system with one measly kiss never would have worked. Something I obviously figured out pretty quickly, but this just proves it.

When we touch, there are sparks.

Hell, maybe even *heart sparks.*

"So, what's after the cook-off tomorrow? Halloween planning?"

Beth blows out a heavy breath and nods. "Yep. Trunk or Treat on Main Street. Instead of delicious chili, I can gorge myself on sugary candy," she jokes.

"What's your favorite?" I ask, eager for more insight into her likes and dislikes, even if it's something as simple as her favorite candy.

"Jolly Ranchers, specifically the watermelon flavor, but I'm happy with whatever I get."

"Not chocolate?" My sister loves mini chocolate bars. Cookies and cream, peanuts, caramel. The kind doesn't matter as long as it's covered, or entirely made of, chocolate.

Beth shakes her head. "Milk chocolate is too sweet for me. I don't mind dark chocolate, but they don't offer much of that for kids at Halloween. Too bitter... What about you?"

"Smarties."

Her nose and forehead wrinkle in disgust.

Laughing, I trace a line down the middle of her forehead before playfully tapping her nose. "Yeah, that's the same reaction my siblings had when they traded their Smarties for my Skittles."

Beth chuckles then moves to take her bowl to the sink, but I stop her with a hand on her arm. "I've got it." Stacking the empty bowl beneath my own after one last slurp of cereal-flavored milk, I bump her knee with mine.

"So, after the cook-off tomorrow, I'm guessing you'll be pretty wiped, but what about Sunday? We could spend it together, then you can join my family for dinner."

The invitation rolls so easily off my tongue, it's like they are meant to be—Beth, me, and my family.

It's strange how *not* freaked out that makes me. Especially since it's serious shit to bring a woman home. And practically unheard of, in my case.

Another first for me.

Her brows shoot skyward. "Really? You want me to meet your family?"

"Well, you already know Kennedy, but yeah... Unless that's too much," I say, suddenly worried that I've gone too far.

Maybe Beth doesn't feel as strong of a connection as I do.

Maybe all she wanted was a wild night with the Suitor's Crossing bad boy; she wouldn't be the first.

Maybe she—

"No, it sounds fun." A bright smile lights up her face, and the unfamiliar spiral I fell into slams to a halt.

Maybe my girl is starting to rub off on me because I've never nervously rambled in my life.

A twinge of unease snakes through my belly.

I'm not sure how I feel about a woman affecting me so easily. *Changing me.* Will it be for better or worse?

CHAPTER TEN

BETH

Suitor's Crossing's Annual Chili Cook-Off marks the official start of fall festivities. Everything becomes pumpkins, gourds, and hay bales until we switch to Christmas mid-November.

It's the perfect opportunity to revel in cooler weather while being warmed by a hearty cup of chili.

Even if this year attendees have to wander outside Hearthstone Lodge's banquet room to experience a chilly autumn breeze rather than ambling down Main Street like usual.

As the town's lead event organizer, I've already sampled a ton of entries into this year's Best Chili contest, and the growing number of donations the fundraiser has received for the fire department assures me that today is a success.

The burst water main may have knocked me down a little, but I recovered, thanks to Kennedy and her family's help, and now I know that if weather ever fails us in the future, we potentially have the perfect back-up solution.

"Hey, how are things going?" Beckett approaches the volunteer table I've been camped behind for the past two hours, and I can't resist casting an appreciative stare over his handsome figure encased in more SCFD paraphernalia.

Several off-duty firefighters are participating in the chili contest to boost the department's visibility and garner those donations, so I'm not surprised that Beckett is also showcasing his association.

"Good. We've met 75% of our fundraising goal, and we've still got a couple more hours to go before shutting down."

"That is awesome!" Beckett's proud smile causes my belly to squeeze and cheeks to flush in pleasure. He looks at me like I singlehandedly saved the fire department's budget. Like I personally donated that much money.

It feels good.

Nice being appreciated for a job well-done.

He raises a hand holding a foam cup. "Speaking of goals, this is our shift's entry for the contest, and the guys think we've got a winner. I'm not sure if you've tried it yet, but I figured I'd bring you a sample, just in case."

"Thanks." I accept the warm cup, shivering at the casual caress of his thumb across mine in the exchange. "I had some earlier, but I'll never say no to food. Obviously." I pat my round stomach with a self-deprecating snicker.

Why the hell did I just point out my flab to the toned fire god in front of me?

Beckett's gray eyes sharpen then deepen to a molten steel color as his gaze drops from my breasts to my belly. "I like a girl who eats. And I like the way you look *and taste*—all soft, sweet curves."

He licks his bottom lip as if he's remembering our night together, where he *did* seem to enjoy burying his face between my thighs, squeezing my love handles, and thoroughly kissing every inch of my body.

"Beckett!" I scold with a light slap to his arm. "This is a family event. Kids are everywhere. What if someone hears you?"

He shrugs, an amused twinkle entering his gaze. "What if they do?"

He lifts a spoonful of chili to his mouth with a smirk. It's a peek at the bad boy rep locals paint him with, until the effect is ruined by a gasp of pain and Beckett frantically chewing then swallowing.

"Holy fuck! Is it supposed to be that spicy?" His chili cup lands on the volunteer table with a thump as he searches for relief.

Swallowing my bite of the same chili, my lips roll inward to hold in a laugh. "Spicy is a relative term," I say as I round the table to the cooler with water bottles we keep on hand for volunteers. "Here, it's not milk, but it should help cool you down."

Beckett guzzles the entire bottle, and I automatically reach for a second one before he asks. That one is demolished just as quickly. Which is what finally breaks my restraint.

Uncontrollable giggles burst free at his cartoonish behavior. Steam should be shooting from his ears and nostrils with the way he's acting.

"You know, for a firefighter, you should be better at handling a little bit of heat," I tease.

"Heat? That wasn't heat. That was fucking lava. How are you not dying right now?" He gestures to my sample cup. The one I keep eating from.

"Guess my spice tolerance is higher than yours, Mr. Fireman."

Beckett pins me to the table with a growl, his arms caging me against the flimsy plastic and metal with ease.

"What did you say earlier? Spice is a relative term? Because I think you may be right." The hard press of his erection nudges between my thighs, and my eyes widen at his blatant arousal.

"How high is your spice tolerance, Beth?" He leans close enough to brush his lips over my ear. "Cayenne and chili peppers are one thing, but what about the bedroom? How *spicy* do you like it there?"

"Umm..." *What the fuck?* How the hell do I answer a question like that in the middle of the *family event* I'm managing! "W-Well..."

"Relax, baby." Beckett retreats with another signature smirk. "I'm just playing with you. I don't expect an answer right now. Too public. But later?" His lips claim mine hard and fast, melting every bone in my body. "Later, I expect an answer."

Later.

The warning makes me all sorts of sweaty and discombobulated. And it only gets worse as the day wears on because Beckett sticks by my side to taunt me with stolen kisses whenever the mood strikes.

After I answer questions from cook-off attendees.

While I sit through judging of the Best Chili contest—where Beckett's crew comes in second.

During the breakdown of the volunteer booth.

By the time I get home hours *later*, my body feels anything but fatigued. Ironic, since Beckett figured I'd be exhausted. Too tired to want to do anything but rest.

Instead, I'm wired.

Hot.

Part of me considers texting Beckett and inviting him over to my place to finish what he started, but I'm not that brave yet.

"Soon, maybe," I comfort myself as I reach for my handy-dandy vibrator to save the day... *or rather, the night.*

Soon, maybe, I'll have the courage to brazenly ask for what I want from Beckett.

Because each time he kisses or compliments me, my confidence grows. Pieces of the armor around my heart crack off, and the caution I usually approach life with takes a backseat to our connection.

A low buzz filters through the covers, and I close my eyes to dream of Beckett and what the future might hold for us.

Until a knock on the front door interrupts my fantasies.

CHAPTER ELEVEN

BECKETT

I shouldn't be here.

I promised to let Beth rest after working so hard today, yet when I got on my motorcycle for a relaxing cruise, I ended up here on her doorstep.

The firehouse is lit up on the other side of the street, and I pray none of the guys see me. They'd give me so much shit if they discovered I'd broken all of my rules for one woman.

Appearing at her house for what could easily be construed as a booty call because I'm so far gone.

"Jesus..." I scrub a hand down my face, not totally recognizing myself at this point, then knock on Beth's door.

If she doesn't answer within five minutes, I leave, I reason.

No need to wake her up if she's already asleep.

Which is a good bet, since there's not a light to be seen through her window curtains.

"You dumb, obsessive..." I turn on my heel, ready to call it a night on this spectacular failure, when the sound of a lock clicks, and the door creeps open.

"Beckett? Is everything alright?"

Beth stands in the doorway outlined by a ray of light coming from the hall behind her. A matching set of burgundy pajamas molds to her curves, and for a moment, I can't speak.

My mind goes completely fucking empty.

"Beckett?" Wariness enters her voice.

It's that note of worry that finally snaps me out of my stupor.

"I know I said I'd let you rest tonight." A frisson of shame settles in my chest, and instinctively, my hand moves to rub it away. "But I had fun with you today, and I decided to go for a ride, and I just wound up here."

Holy fucking shit!

Now, I'm morphing into an anxious mess.

Hopefully, she finds it as endearing on me as I find it on her.

"Oh... Do you want to come in?" Beth steps back and motions me inside.

"Yeah, *in* is good. *In* is great," I babble nonsensically.

What suspiciously looks like an amused smile tugs at the edges of Beth's mouth.

"Do you want a drink or...?"

"I didn't wake you, did I?"

She bites her lip as a scarlet flush blooms on her cheeks and chest.

Aww, hell, I definitely woke her up.

"No, I wasn't sleeping. I..." Her head turns toward a bedroom where the corner of a bed and dresser are in view.

She fidgets on one foot then the other before seeming to arrive at some internal decision, because when she faces me again, a mischievous resolve has erased her hesitancy.

"Why don't you come see for yourself?"

Confused but willing to follow her lead, I trail her steps into the bedroom, the air drenched in her familiar rose scent.

Beth slowly climbs onto the bed and lays back with her head propped against a pillow. The scene would be innocent except for the provocative way her legs fall open to reveal a dark wet spot at the seam of her sleep shorts.

"What were you doing, naughty girl?" My eyes snag on the purple vibrator on her nightstand, and pieces start falling into place.

My girl wasn't tired.

She was horny.

And I'm the genius—*i.e. lucky bastard*—who got here just in time to help her out.

My tongue clucks in admonishment as I strip down to nothing. Shirt, jeans, boots? I don't need them to take care of my girl.

"Beth, were you gonna play with that sweet pussy all by yourself? You should have called me."

"I thought about it," she rasps, watching my every move.

Grabbing the toy, my thumb flips the switch to turn it on, then I press a separate button to cycle through its vibration modes. I choose a gentler setting to start then glance at my girl, who's practically panting with excitement.

"On your knees, baby. Hands on the headboard," I command.

Beth licks her lips then complies, her round ass jiggling under the flimsy material of her shorts.

Once she's in position, I climb behind her until the back of her thighs rest on the top of mine and her ass is cradling my hard cock.

"Hmm... This won't do," I *tsk* before working her shorts lower so they rest beneath her peachy cheeks, giving me access to what I want while still trapping her legs together.

Leaning forward, I whisper in her ear, "That's better, isn't it?"

"Y-Yeah...!" Her stuttering affirmation ends in a yelp when I nestle the vibrator between her slick folds. The toy easily glides from her dripping cunt to her clit, and it's the hottest fucking thing I've ever seen or heard.

"Fuck, baby, do you hear how juicy this little pussy is? You thinking of me while you were soaking these sheets with all this cream?"

A jerky nod titters from her.

"I always think of you," she admits, and I swear my heart stops in my chest at the confession.

"That's good, baby. I'm the only man you need. I'll satisfy this greedy little cunt. You don't ever have to worry about that."

My hungry tongue laps at her neck before I suck hard enough to leave a mark.

A symbol of my promise and possession.

Soon, Beth cries out with the crash of her first climax of the evening, but it won't be the last.

Feral for more, I work my dick between her squishy thighs, loving the warm give of them, as the head of my cock kisses her wet entrance.

"It's gonna be a tight fit like this, baby. You ready?"

"Yes... Yes, Beckett. Give me more."

I plunge forward with a harsh grunt and grit my teeth when her hot sheath constricts around me.

"Shit!" The vibrator wobbles in my hand, but I recover and shift it so her clit gets the brunt of the vibrating waves, while my cock fucks into Beth's pussy. "I'll give you more, baby. I'll give you everything."

The declaration should scare the hell out of me, but I'm too focused on ruining Beth for any other man.

Too obsessed with the bounce of her generous curves and screams of pleasure as she comes again.

Too *wrecked* by this beautiful woman as my own orgasm erupts to do anything but thank god, she's *mine*.

CHAPTER TWELVE

BETH

Beckett's grandfather wraps me in a warm hug the moment I step into his cabin for the weekly Caldwell dinner.

"It's nice to finally meet you, Beth. Kennedy has mentioned how talented you are, and she's not the first one to sing your praises."

"Oh, well, thank you." I had no idea people knew who I was.

Minor City Hall employees don't warrant as much attention and name recognition as someone like the mayor or a city councilperson. At least, not in my experience at my old job.

"She's amazing, right?" Beckett's hand lands on my hip and tugs me into his side for a quick peck to my temple.

I wouldn't have pegged him for a PDA kind of guy, but he's been surprising me at every turn, so maybe I need to let all of my preconceived notions about him go.

Forget about the bad boy reputation I've heard around town.

The one that made me originally call our hook-up a one-night stand.

Because the flirting at the cook-off happened.

Then last night—literally the kind of intimacy I've dreamed of—destroyed my reservations.

Then there was today.

A day spent exploring with Beckett. Wandering down the Main Street shops. Enjoying meals at Crossing's Cups & Cakes and Daffodil's.

He even took me to the infamous Suitor's Crossing bridge where *heart sparks* originated!

That's not a casual move.

Especially when it culminates in an invitation to a private family dinner.

Right?

Kennedy is up next for a hug, her curious gaze bouncing between me and her brother. "This is unexpected but not unwelcome," she whispers in my ear. "I'm happy you're here."

"Me, too." Though I'm a little embarrassed about springing my relationship with her brother on her.

Does forty-eight hours of sex, fun, and flirting qualify as a relationship?

"Alright, Ken, let the rest of us say hello to Beckett's girl." Soren, the eldest sibling, joins our growing group in the living room, and a flush of self-consciousness sweeps over my cheeks.

Am I Beckett's girl?

I'd like to be, but a one-sided crush is all I've had for months.

It takes two people for that claim to work—me, the willing claimee, and Beckett, the willing claimant.

He seems pretty damn willing...

"Don't crush her, you big lug," Beckett jokes as his brother wraps me in his burly arms.

We all laugh, and I accept hugs from the rest of the Caldwells, before we settle at a large dining table where numerous mismatched chairs have been added to accommodate the siblings' partners.

It's a tight fit but cozy all the same.

And I cross my fingers under the table that this is a glimpse at something permanent—a life full of love and family that I get to call mine.

CHAPTER THIRTEEN

BECKETT

I watch Beth through the kitchen window as she laughs with my brothers and Gramps around the firepit. Dinner has been devoured, and now everyone is ready to enjoy the beautiful fall weather and some s'mores.

Everyone except for my sister.

Kennedy joins me at the kitchen sink, where I volunteered for dish duty, and motions to the group outside.

"Makes for a pretty picture..." Her elbow digs into my ribs. "Beth's different for you, but I like that, and you do, too, huh?"

Her smug words shatter the carefree facade I've been wearing all evening, so I don't respond, just keep looking out the window and scrubbing a sponge over the same damn plate.

Maybe she'll take the hint.

"Oh, yeah, you definitely do," she says, ignoring the hint completely.

"You don't know what you're talking about." I refuse to acknowledge how right she is.

Because I absolutely do not need relationship advice from my little sister.

"Really? Your eyes haven't left her from the moment you guys arrived." She crosses her arms over her chest and faces me. "I'm guessing you've never felt this way before, and it probably confuses the hell out of you. Close enough?"

I shrug.

What can I say? She's right.

I haven't understood a damn thing happening to me since Beth crashed into my life. All I know is that I want her to be happy. Taken care of. And, as selfish as it is, I want to be the man who makes all of that happen for her.

Which makes no damn sense.

Because I'm not that guy. I never have been.

Until one woman changed everything.

"Mind your business, sis," I say with little heat then escape outside. The rest of the dishes will have to wait as Kennedy's knowing laughter dogs my footsteps.

Footsteps that lead straight to Beth.

Looping an arm over her shoulders, I hug her close. "Are you having a good time?"

"Yeah, your family is great." Her smile beams up at me, and my heart stutters then thumps to life again with a painful throb. *Goddammit.* I'm so fucking screwed.

"They're also a lot. Do you want to get out of here?" I ask, suddenly desperate to get her alone.

The weight of my family's speculative stares is a vise around my lungs. They see too much. Know me too well.

Realize the significance of bringing Beth here.

When I don't even think Beth understands the importance of her presence.

Her face falls as she bites her lip and nods. "Sure. Let me say goodbye to everyone."

A round of hugs and farewells take place before we're in my truck and driving aimlessly back to the main part of town.

My synapses are in overdrive.

My heart is pumping blood like crazy, and I rub a hand over my chest to dissipate the burn.

"Is everything okay?" A small voice floats from the passenger seat.

I know my weird behavior is freaking Beth out, but it's hard for me to put into words what's going on. Not when I barely understand it myself.

"Yep," I clip, then frown at the snappish tone. "Sorry, I'm fine. Just thinking."

"About what?"

The turn for Oak Park and the famous Suitor's Crossing bridge appears on our right, and on impulse, I signal and pull down the gravel lane to the parking lot, despite the fact that we were here earlier.

Silence fills the truck cabin once the engine shuts off.

Silence but for the harsh exhales pushing through my lips.

"Beckett?"

"*Heart sparks*," I blurt out.

What the hell?

I scrub a hand over my face and groan.

"What about *heart sparks*?"

Meeting Beth's eyes in the shadowy truck cab, a world of excuses pops into my head. Reasons for *heart sparks* being on my mind. Like how we're yards away from the Suitor's Crossing bridge where they originated. The legend of love and soulmates is so close that of course I can't help thinking about it.

Except that's not entirely true.

"Beth... I like you. A lot." Inhaling a shuddering breath, I plunge forward, praying I don't regret diving headfirst into this. "I haven't been able to stop thinking about you since that first moment at City Hall. I've never been a huge believer in *heart sparks*, but damn, if you don't make me feel like they're as real as us sitting here under the moonlight."

"But I thought you didn't do relationships," she says blankly, twisting in her seat to face me. "This is a fling."

The words are so hesitant. Unsure. I wonder if she even believes what she's saying.

"Is that why we spent today together? Is that why I loved waking up with your head on my chest this morning? Is a fling what you want?" A nerve pinches near my heart at the possibility.

"No. I want what my friends have. I want love." She ducks her head, her hair spilling over her shoulder to hide the blush I'm sure is staining her cheeks.

My finger brushes below her chin to tilt her gaze up to meet mine.

"Don't hide from me. Wanting love isn't something to be ashamed of."

"Of course not, but we've only had one official date and a few hook-ups. It's too soon to bring up love."

"I'm the one who brought up *heart sparks*," I point out.

"Because you think I'm yours? Your... soulmate?" Cautious hope shines in her eyes.

"I don't know. Maybe. This is the closest I've ever felt to love and forever. *You* are the closest I've ever felt to those things. Are you willing to see this through? Are you willing to take a chance on me?"

A scoff of laughter bubbles from her chest before she covers her lips.

"Sorry, when I'm nervous I laugh. Ramble and laugh... Oh, god, I'm doing it again." She stops and takes a deep breath.

"Love is what I've yearned for from the moment I moved to Suitor's Crossing. Caroline, Amelie... They took risks and found love. *Heart sparks* found them when they least expected it. Truthfully, I've been envious of their good fortune, even if it makes me a bad friend."

"You're not a bad friend," I defend her automatically.

A self-deprecating smile hooks along one side of her mouth. "Thanks, but that's beside the point. What I'm trying to say is that yes, I'm willing to see where this goes. I've had a crush on you for months."

"My little stalker," I tease.

"Oh, god, shut up." She playfully pushes at my shoulder, but I don't let it stop me from leaning forward and capturing her lips with mine. Relishing the sweet taste of my girl.

"I like that you're obsessed with me, baby. It makes me feel like I'm not alone in this crazy obsession I have for you."

"You're definitely not, and now I don't have to feel guilty for staring so much when you train outside the fire department."

Chuckling, I brush my thumb over her bottom lip. "I'll be sure to put on a good show for you. It's only fair since I love watching you, too."

And touching her.

And kissing her.

I want everything with my curvy little rambler.

I may not know the first thing about love, relationships, and forever, but with Beth by my side, I'm confident I'll figure it out.

There's no other choice when she's my *heart spark*.

EPILOGUE

BETH

ONE YEAR LATER

The rumble of motorcycles fills the air before engines cut off and nature's song slowly returns to the idyllic space. Our book club decided that today would be perfect for a ride through the mountains with our men before stopping for a picnic at one of the scenic overlooks.

Reaper's Wolves MC guys unpack food and drinks with the help of my friends and a few biker bunnies who hang out at the clubhouse. The only one missing from our group is Kat, who insisted she already had plans, though I wonder if she just didn't want to feel like the eleventh wheel as the single girl out.

Not that every MC guy or biker bunny is paired up, but our core book club is, and I worry Kat feels like she doesn't fit in anymore.

"Hey, you okay?" Beckett reaches back to squeeze my thigh.

I should probably unwrap myself from where I cling to his muscular form after an exhilarating ride on the back of his motorcycle. Instead, I cling tighter and sigh.

"Yeah... Just concerned about Kat."

He removes his helmet then tips his head to the side so our eyes meet.

Understanding washes through the silver. I've shared how lonely and out of place I felt last year during book club, so he's aware of why I empathize so much with Kat.

"You've got a good heart, baby." His hands carefully unlatch my helmet and set it aside before pressing a soft kiss to my frowning mouth. "Kat will find someone. Maybe you can help her out. I've got plenty of single friends."

He wags his eyebrows suggestively knowing just how to brighten my mood.

Easing off the bike, I shake my head. "No way. I tried matchmaking before when I set Caroline up on that blind date. What a disaster that turned out to be."

When she'd shared how rude Tyler had been that night, horror and rage had bled through me. I thought I'd vetted him enough, but he'd proven me wrong.

Proved why I was right to be so cautious in every aspect of my life.

"It wasn't a total disaster," Beckett says. He points toward Caroline and Snow, whose arms are looped around her waist as he peppers kisses over her giggling face. "They met again that night, right?"

"Happy coincidence... Anyway, I'll text Kat later to check on her." Grabbing Beckett's hand, I pull him away from the motorcycle, so we can join the others, noticing Ranger and Grim's sister off by themselves near a grill.

Wonder when that will officially become a thing...

"Such a good friend." Beckett tickles my side with a mischievous smile. "That's why I love you so much."

"Oh, is that why? I thought it was because—" My mouth slams shut when I realize I was about to blurt out something wholly inappropriate.

Beckett's grin widens. "Because what?"

"Never mind," I evade, turning my nose up at his knowing inquiry. "You're such a bad influence."

"And that's why *you* love *me*," he growls and spins me around until I bump into his chest with an *oomph*.

As Beckett bends me over his arm to kiss me senseless—a shout of whoops rising behind us from our friends—I concede to his possession.

Because I *do* love him.

The former bad boy of Suitor's Crossing.

My very own *heart spark*.

***

Did you love Beckett and Beth? Tell me your favorite scene here[1]!

***

Don't miss the final Caldwell sibling finding love in *Griffen the Mountain Man*[2]!

---

1. https://forms.gle/24SdnUUCBNikX1Pw7

2. https://www.amazon.com/Griffen-Mountain-Man-Crossing-Caldwells-ebook/dp/B0FQPRTKD6

THANKS FOR READING & DON'T FORGET TO RATE/ REVIEW!

Please consider leaving a rating/review. Ratings & reviews are the #1 way to support an indie author like me.

Also, don't miss out on free books and up-to-date release information. You can sign up for my newsletter here[1].

I appreciate your support!

XO, Hallie

1. https://www.thearrowedheart.com/hallie-bennett

ABOUT THE AUTHOR

Hallie prefers steamy, insta-love stories where curvy girls are claimed by filthy-talking heroes. And when she ran out of reading material, she decided to write her own stories. If you want a quick, hot read, she's your girl!